This book belongs to

Franklin's Giant Treasury

Franklin

Franklin is a trademark of Kids Can Press Ltd.

Franklin's Giant Treasury

© 2002 Context*x* Inc. and Brenda Clark Illustrator Inc.

This book includes the following stories:
Franklin in the Dark first published in 1986
Hurry Up, Franklin first published in 1989
Franklin Fibs first published in 1991
Franklin Is Bossy first published in 1993
Franklin Goes to School first published in 1995
Franklin's School Play first published in 1997
Franklin's Class Trip first published in 1999
Franklin's Neighborhood first published in 1999

All text © 1986, 1989, 1991, 1993, 1995, 1997, 1999 Context*x* Inc.
All illustrations © 1986, 1989, 1991, 1993, 1995, 1997, 1999
Brenda Clark Illustrator Inc.

Franklin's Class Trip written by Paulette Bourgeois and Sharon Jennings.
Franklin's Neighborhood written by Sharon Jennings.
Franklin Goes to School interior illustrations prepared with the assistance
of Dimitrije Kostic.
Franklin's School Play, Franklin's Class Trip and *Franklin's Neighborhood*
interior illustrations prepared with the assistance of Shelley Southern.

Kids Can Press acknowledges the financial support of the Ontario Arts Council,
the Canada Council for the Arts and the Government of Canada, through the
BPIDP, for our publishing activity.

Published in Canada by
Kids Can Press Ltd.
29 Birch Avenue
Toronto, ON M4V 1E2

Published in the U.S. by
Kids Can Press Ltd.
2250 Military Road
Tonawanda, NY 14150

www.kidscanpress.com

Printed in Hong Kong, China, by Wing King Tong Company Limited

CM 02 0 9 8 7 6 5 4 3 2 1

National Library of Canada Cataloguing in Publication Data

Bourgeois, Paulette
    Franklin's giant treasury / Paulette Bourgeois, Brenda Clark.

Complete contents: *Franklin in the dark – Hurry up, Franklin – Franklin fibs –
Franklin is bossy – Franklin goes to school – Franklin's school play – Franklin's
class trip – Franklin's neighborhood.*

ISBN 1-55337-558-0

I. Clark, Brenda   II. Title.

PS8553.O85477F856 2002   jC813'.54   C2002-902208-8
PZ7

Kids Can Press is a *corus*™ Entertainment company

Franklin's
GIANT
Treasury

Paulette Bourgeois • Brenda Clark

Kids Can Press

Contents

Franklin in the Dark

FRANKLIN could slide down a riverbank all by himself. He could count forwards and backwards. He could even zip zippers and button buttons. But Franklin was afraid of small, dark places and that was a problem because...

Franklin was a turtle. He was afraid of crawling into his small, dark shell. And so, Franklin the turtle dragged his shell behind him.

Every night, Franklin's mother would take a flashlight and shine it into his shell.

"See," she would say, "there's nothing to be afraid of."

She always said that. She wasn't afraid of anything. But Franklin was sure that creepy things, slippery things, and monsters lived inside his small, dark shell.

So Franklin went looking for help. He walked until he met a duck.

"Excuse me, Duck. I'm afraid of small, dark places and I can't crawl inside my shell. Can you help me?"

"Maybe," quacked the duck. "You see, I'm afraid of very deep water. Sometimes, when nobody is watching, I wear my water wings. Would my water wings help you?"

"No," said Franklin. "I'm not afraid of water."

So Franklin walked and walked until he met a lion.

"Excuse me, Lion. I'm afraid of small, dark places and I can't crawl inside my shell. Can you help me?"

"Maybe," roared the lion. "You see, I'm afraid of great, loud noises. Sometimes, when nobody is looking, I wear my earmuffs. Would my earmuffs help you?"

"No," said Franklin. "I'm not afraid of great, loud noises."

So Franklin walked and walked and walked
until he met a bird.

"Excuse me, Bird. I'm afraid of small, dark
places and I can't crawl inside my shell. Can you
help me?"

"Maybe," chirped the bird. "I'm afraid of flying
so high that I get dizzy and fall to the ground.
Sometimes, when nobody is looking, I pull my
parachute. Would my parachute help you?"

"No," said Franklin. "I'm not afraid of flying
high and getting dizzy."

So Franklin walked and walked and walked and walked until he met a polar bear.

"Excuse me, Polar Bear. I'm afraid of small, dark places and I can't crawl inside my shell. Can you help me?"

"Maybe," growled the bear. "You see, I'm afraid of freezing on icy, cold nights. Sometimes, when nobody is looking, I wear my snowsuit to bed. Would my snowsuit help you?"

"No," said Franklin. "I'm not afraid of freezing on icy, cold nights."

Franklin was tired and hungry. He walked and walked and walked until he met his mother.

"Oh, Franklin. I was so afraid you were lost."

"You were afraid? I didn't know mothers were ever afraid," said Franklin.

24

"Well, did you find some help?" she asked.
"No. I met a duck who was afraid of deep
water."
"Hmmm," she said.

"Then I met a lion who was afraid of great, loud noises."

"Uh, hmmmm," she said.

"And then I met a bird who was afraid of falling and a polar bear who was afraid of freezing."

"Oh," she said. "They were all afraid of something."

"Hmmmm," said Franklin.

It was getting late. Franklin was very tired and very hungry. They walked and walked until they were home.

Franklin's mother gave him a cold supper and a warm hug. And then she sent him off to bed. "Goodnight, dear," she said.

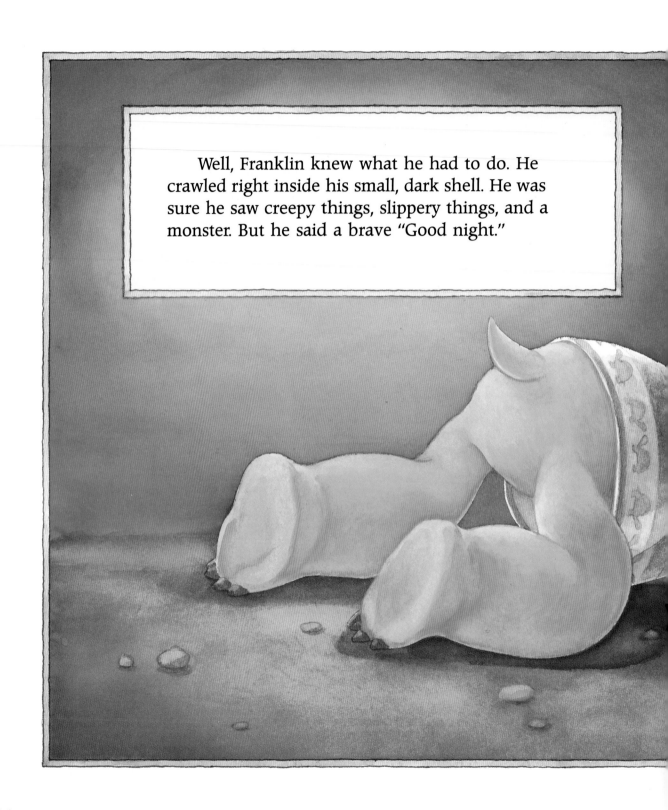

Well, Franklin knew what he had to do. He crawled right inside his small, dark shell. He was sure he saw creepy things, slippery things, and a monster. But he said a brave "Good night."

And then, when nobody was looking, Franklin the turtle turned on his night light.

Hurry Up, Franklin

FRANKLIN could slide down a river bank all by himself. He could count forwards and backwards. He could zip zippers and button buttons. He could even sleep alone in his small, dark shell. But Franklin was slow…

Even for a turtle.

"Hurry up, Franklin," pleaded his mother. "Hurry up, Franklin," begged his father. "Hurry up, Franklin," shouted his friends.

"I'll be there in a minute," said Franklin. But there was always so much to see and so much to do. Franklin was never there in just a minute.

One day Franklin was very excited. He was going to Bear's house. It was a special day. A very special day. "Hurry up," said Franklin's mother. "You can't be late."

It wasn't far to Bear's house. Just along the
path, over the bridge and across the berry patch.
Franklin meant to hurry—except he saw something
unusual. He wandered off the path and found
Rabbit bobbing up and down in the tall, green
grass.

"What are you doing?" Franklin asked Rabbit.

"Playing Leap Frog," said Rabbit. "Do you
want to play with me?"

"I'm on my way to Bear's house," said Franklin.
"And I can't be late."

"There's lots of time," said Rabbit, forgetting
that Franklin was slow, even for a turtle. "It's just
along the path, over the bridge and across the
berry patch. Come and play with me."

Franklin knew it wasn't far and so he said yes. Rabbit leaped over Franklin again and again. But after a while Rabbit said, "It's time to go. Hurry up, Franklin, or you'll be late." Then Rabbit bounded along the path on his way to Bear's house.

"I'll be there in a minute," said Franklin. And
he meant to be there in just a minute – except he
heard an odd sound. Franklin wandered even
farther off the path until he found Otter sliding up
and down the river bank.

"What are you doing?" Franklin asked Otter.

"Slipping and sliding," answered Otter. "Do
you want to play with me?"

"I'm on my way to Bear's house," said Franklin.
"And I can't be late."

"There's lots of time," said Otter, forgetting
that Franklin was slow, even for a turtle. "It's just
along the path, over the bridge and across the
berry patch. Come and play with me."

Franklin knew it wasn't far and so he said yes. Franklin slid down the river bank and splashed and blew bubbles until Otter said, "It's time to go. Hurry up, Franklin, or you'll be late." Then Otter swam away with a flick of her tail on her way to Bear's house.

"I'll be there in a minute," said Franklin.

It was very quiet. Franklin was alone and far from the path. Rabbit had gone. Otter had gone. Franklin had a frightening thought. Maybe he was already too late!

Franklin walked as fast as his turtle legs could walk. He hurried through the fields and along the path. He was almost at the bridge when he heard a rustle in the grass and saw a patch of reddish fur. It was Fox, hiding in the brush.

"Do you want to play with me?" asked Fox.

"I have to hurry," said Franklin. "I'm on my way to Bear's house!"

"It's not very far," said Fox. "Just over the bridge and across the berry patch. Come and play hide and seek."

Franklin hesitated. Hide and seek was his favourite game.

"Ready or not?" asked Fox.

Franklin shouted, "Ready!" And he was just about to step off the path when he remembered it was a very special day and he couldn't be late.

"I can't play," said Franklin. "I have to hurry."

Franklin rushed along the path and over the bridge. He was in such a hurry that he almost stepped on Snail.

"Where are you going in such a hurry?" asked Snail, who was even slower than Franklin.

"I'm on my way to Bear's house," said Franklin. "I have to hurry. I can't be late. Being late would ruin everything."

Snail began to cry.

"What's wrong?" asked Franklin.

"I'll never get to Bear's house on time," sobbed Snail.

"It's not very far," said Franklin. "Just across the berry patch."

It seemed very far to Snail, and he sobbed even harder.

"Don't worry," said Franklin bravely. But even Franklin was worried. It was farther than he thought. It was a very big berry patch. He wished he hadn't played with Rabbit. He wished he hadn't played with Otter. He wished he hadn't wasted so much time talking to Fox. Then he remembered it was Bear's special day. There was no time to cry. He had to hurry.

"Come along, Snail," said Franklin, helping
Snail slide onto his back.

"Please hurry," whispered Snail. But Franklin
needed no urging. He moved surely and steadily.
He hurried past the blackberries. He hurried past
the gooseberries. He even hurried past the
raspberries. And he was almost at Bear's front gate
when he remembered something important.

He stopped right there at the edge of the berry patch and started picking handfuls of the ripest, plumpest, juiciest blueberries in the berry patch.

"We don't have time to pick berries," said Snail. "You know we can't be late."

Franklin whispered into Snail's right ear. And soon Snail was helping too. They picked until the bush was clean.

"Hurry up," said Snail. "Please hurry up, Franklin."

He hurried up Bear's path, through the front door, across the kitchen and into Bear's living room.

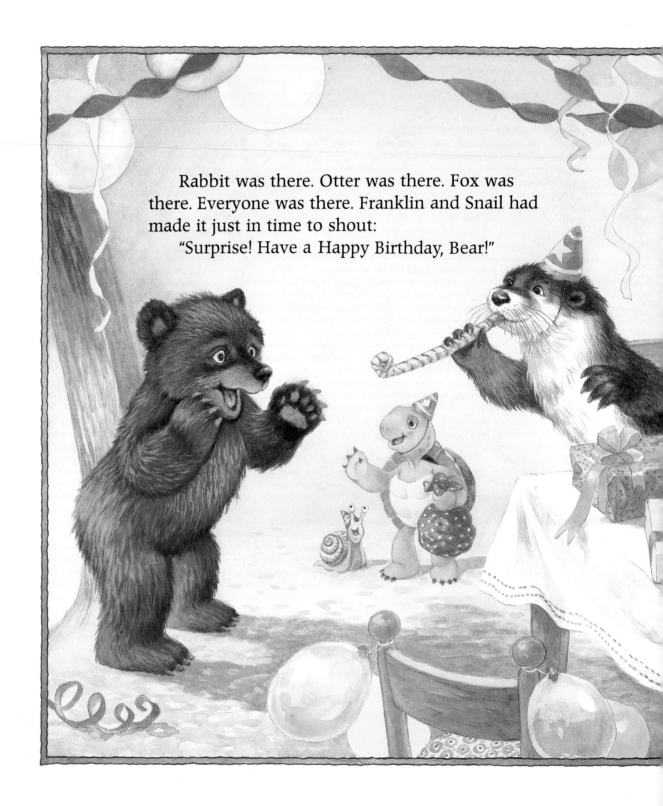

Rabbit was there. Otter was there. Fox was there. Everyone was there. Franklin and Snail had made it just in time to shout:

"Surprise! Have a Happy Birthday, Bear!"

And he did.

Franklin Fibs

FRANKLIN could slide down a riverbank all by himself. He could count forwards and backwards. He could zip zippers and button buttons. He could even tie shoe laces, but Franklin could not swallow seventy-six flies in the blink of an eye.

And that was a problem because Franklin said he could. He told all his friends he could. Franklin had fibbed.

It started with Bear.
Bear boasted, "I can climb the highest tree."
He scrambled to the tip of a pine.

Then Hawk bragged, "I can fly over the berry patch without flapping my wings."

He soared over the woods and past the berry patch without ruffling a feather.

75

Beaver crowed, "I can chop down a tree with just my teeth."

Beaver gnawed first on one side, then on the other. Chips of wood flew this way and that. The tree crashed down.

"And," she said, "I can make my own dam."

Franklin couldn't climb a tree. He couldn't chop down a tree. He couldn't fly. And he forgot everything he *could* do. So he fibbed.

"I can swallow seventy-six flies in the blink of an eye," he said.

His friends were astounded.

"Watch me," said Franklin.

Franklin gobbled two, four, six flies.

"There!"

"But that was only six flies," said Hawk.

"There were only six flies flying," said Franklin. "And I ate them all in the blink of an eye. I could have eaten seventy more."

"Let's see," said Beaver.

Franklin frowned. There was no way he could eat seventy-six flies in the blink of an eye. No way at all.

Franklin had no appetite at dinner.
"What's wrong?" asked his mother.
"I can't eat seventy-six flies in the blink of an eye."
"Neither can I," said Franklin's father.
"Neither can I," said Franklin's mother.
"But you don't have to," said Franklin sadly.

"And I do." Franklin told them all about the flies. His mother nodded and his father hmmmmed.

"You have quite an imagination," said Franklin's father.

The next morning, Franklin's friends were waiting. Beaver had a surprise.

"Eat them," she dared.

Franklin wrapped a woolly winter scarf twice around his neck. "Can't," he squawked. "I have a sore throat."

His friends laughed.

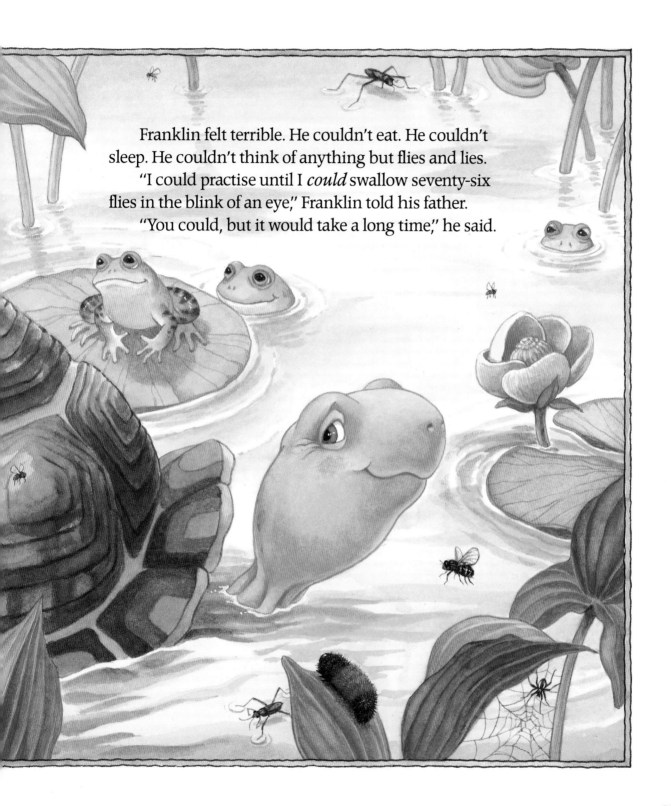

Franklin felt terrible. He couldn't eat. He couldn't sleep. He couldn't think of anything but flies and lies.

"I could practise until I *could* swallow seventy-six flies in the blink of an eye," Franklin told his father.

"You could, but it would take a long time," he said.

"I could stop playing with my friends," Franklin told his mother.

"You could, but you might be lonely," she said.

"I could tell them I fibbed," said Franklin.

"You could do that," said Franklin's parents. "And then you can show them what you *can* do."

The next day, Franklin's friends were waiting.

"I can't eat seventy-six flies in the blink of an eye," admitted Franklin.

"We guessed," said Bear.

"But," said Franklin, "I *can* eat seventy-six flies."

Franklin's friends sighed.

"Really," said Franklin.

Franklin ran home.

He got the flies, a bowl, some flour, milk, eggs and honey. He poured and stirred, rolled and baked. Finally, he was ready.

94

"Watch me!" Franklin gobbled the entire fly pie.

"There," said Franklin licking his lips.

"Amazing! What else can you do?" asked Beaver.

Franklin swaggered with success. He was about to say that he could eat two fly pies in a gulp.

Then he thought twice and said nothing at all.
Even a turtle gets tired of eating fly pie.

Franklin Is Bossy

FRANKLIN the turtle could zip zippers and button buttons. He could count by twos and tie his shoes. He had lots of friends and one best friend, named Bear. They played tag and marbles, hopscotch and ball. But one day something awful happened. Franklin and Bear had a fight.

It was a steamy summer morning. Franklin told his friends, "Let's play marbles." And they did.

After a while, Franklin said, "I'm tired of marbles, let's have a race."

"You always pick the games," grumbled Bear.
Franklin paid no attention.
They started to run. Bear was in the lead.
Goose followed close behind. Franklin saw that he
was losing and cried out ...

"Slowest one wins!" as he crawled across the finish line last.

"That's not fair," said Bear.

Franklin ignored him. "I'm tired of running, let's play baseball."

Bear did not put on his mitt. He did not put
on his cap. He was mad.

"It's too hot. I don't want to play," said Bear.

"Me neither," said Beaver.

"It's not too hot!" said Franklin.

"Is too," said Bear.

"Is not," said Franklin.

"I don't want to play with you, Franklin!"
shouted Bear.

"And I don't want to play with you, either!"
Franklin shouted back.

Franklin stomped all the way home.

"What's wrong?" asked his father.

"There's no one to play with," answered Franklin.

"Maybe your friends will come by later," said Franklin's father.

"Maybe," he said.

In his room, Franklin built a castle. He made a cape to be brave in. He made shields and swords and suits of armour. He drew pictures. He played house. He read stories. He played by himself for one whole hour, and then he didn't know what to do.

So, Franklin went looking for company.
His friends were in the river, cooling off.
"Are you still hot?" he asked.
"No," they answered.
"Then let's play ball," said Franklin.

Before anyone had a chance to say a word,
Franklin started giving orders. "Bear, you play first
base. Goose and Beaver, you go to the outfield.
I'll be the pitcher."

"No way!" shouted Bear. "I don't want to play
with you. You are too bossy."

All of Franklin's friends nodded.

"Bear's right," they said.

Franklin turned his back and went home.

There was no one to play with and nothing much to do. So, he helped his father all afternoon. They weeded the garden and washed the floors. And they made supper for Mole because he was sick.

"You're a good friend," Mole told Franklin's father.

On the way home, Franklin asked, "Do you and Mole have fights?"

"Sometimes," said Franklin's father. "But we always make up."

119

Franklin played alone for another whole day.
He missed Bear and all his friends. And he had
lots of time to think.
    He would go to Bear and apologize.
    Franklin and Bear met on the bridge.

"I was going to your house," said Franklin.
"And I was going to your house," said Bear.
"I'm sorry," said Franklin. "It was all my fault."
"No, it was my fault," said Bear.
"Mine," said Franklin.
"No, mine," said Bear.

"STOP!" shouted Beaver, who was listening under the bridge.

"This is silly!" Beaver slapped her tail so hard that Franklin and Bear jumped. They started to giggle.

"Friends?" asked Franklin.
"Friends," said Bear.

Beaver wanted to play baseball. Bear and Goose and Duck agreed. They were picking teams when Franklin insisted on being the pitcher ... again.

All together his friends shouted, "No fair, Franklin!"

Franklin knew they were right. He couldn't always be pitcher. It was his turn to play in the outfield.

And it wasn't so bad, for although Franklin
didn't catch a single ball ... he did catch lots of flies.

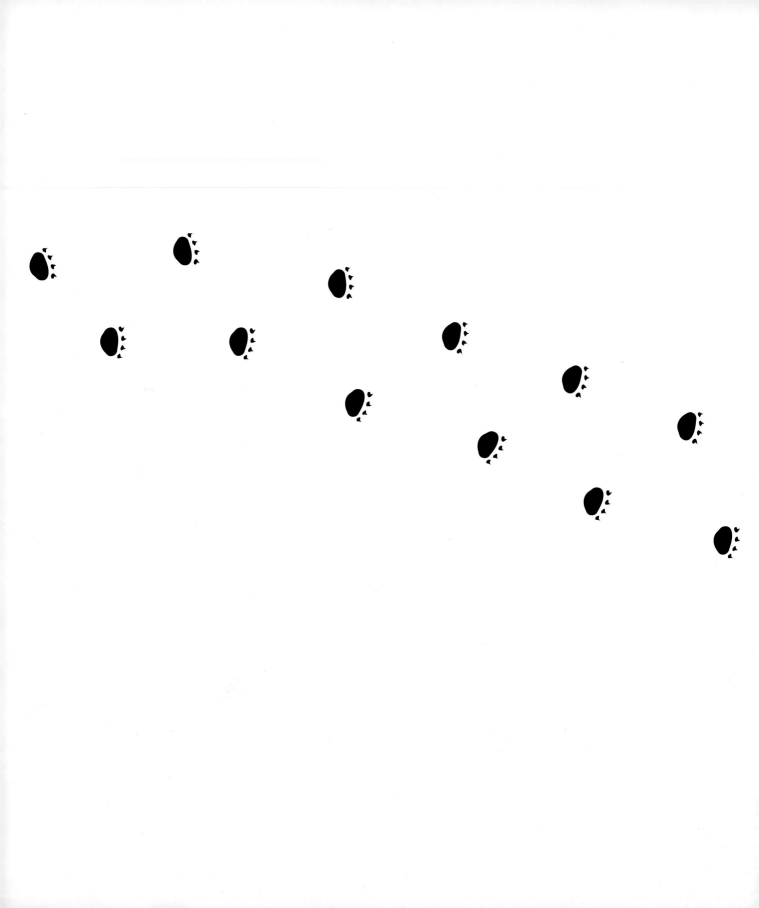

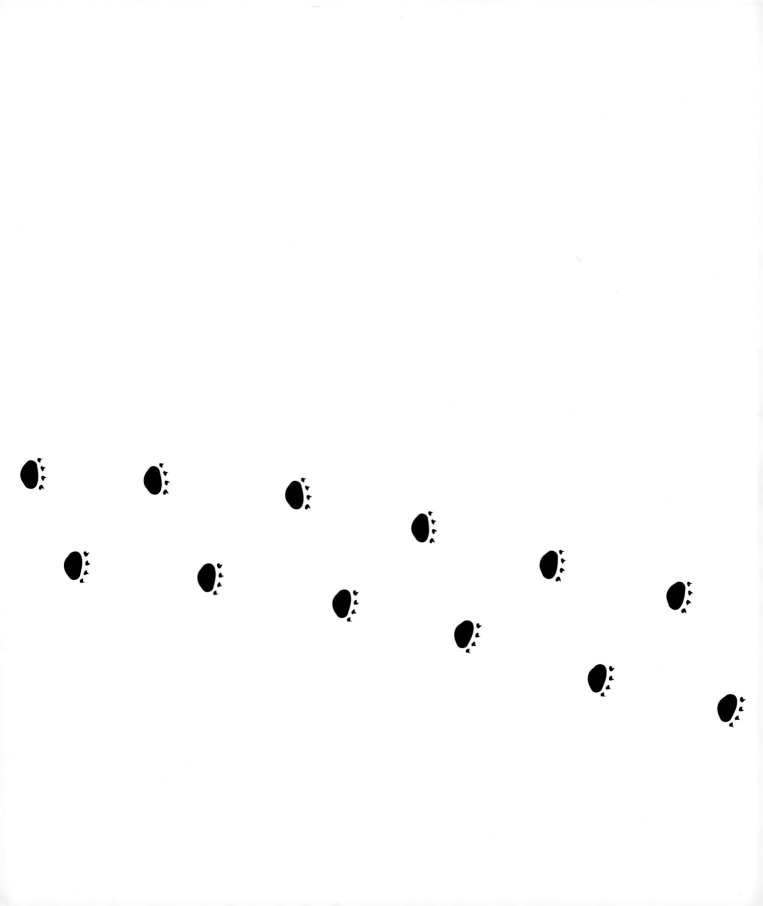

❧ Franklin's ❧
GIANT
Treasury
Part II

Contents

Franklin Goes to School

FRANKLIN could count by twos and tie his shoes. He could zip zippers and button buttons. But Franklin was worried about starting school. And that was a problem because Franklin was going to school for the very first time.

Franklin woke up with the sun. "It's my first day of school!" he told Goldie, his fish.

Franklin packed his new pencil case with a ruler, a pencil, an eraser and twelve colored pencils that he had sharpened himself.

Then he woke his parents.

141

"Hurry," he said to his parents. "I cannot be late for school."

Franklin's mother looked at the clock. "Even the teacher is not awake," she laughed. "It is too early."

"You must be very excited," said Franklin's father. Franklin nodded.

It was so early that there was time to make a big breakfast.

"You'll need a full tummy to work at school," said Franklin's father.

Franklin was not hungry. "I already have a full tummy," he said. "It feels like it is full of jumping frogs."

Franklin's mother gave him a hug. "I felt that way on my first day of school. But the funny feeling went away."

Franklin ate a little. He double-checked his book bag. Finally it was time to go to school.

Halfway to the bus stop, Franklin clutched his tummy.

"I don't want to go," he said.

Franklin's father gave him a hug. "That's how I felt when I started school," he said. "Look. All your friends are waiting for the bus."

There was a big crowd at the bus stop. There were brothers and sisters and mothers and fathers.

Beaver was carrying her favorite book.

"I can read it," she said.

"All of it?" asked Bear.

"Yes," she answered proudly.

Franklin rubbed his tummy.

Rabbit pulled out a brand-new notebook.

"My big sister showed me how to write my numbers," he said.

"All of them?" asked Fox.

"Most of them," boasted Rabbit.

Franklin looked at his mother. "I want to go home," he said.

"We will be here after school to hear about all the things you did today," she said.

152

When the bus arrived, Rabbit grabbed his sister's hand and climbed aboard. Bear stood on the steps and waved good-bye again and again. Franklin hugged his mother, then his father. He kept hugging even after his friends had found seats.

As the bus pulled away, Franklin looked out the window. He didn't know if he was ready for school.

"Do you think the teacher will yell?" wondered Rabbit, who jumped at loud noises.

"Do you think there's a bathroom at school?" asked Beaver, fidgeting in her seat.

"I hope somebody has an extra snack," said Bear, who had already eaten his.

Franklin did not say anything. The bus ride seemed very, very long.

When they arrived, their teacher was waiting.

Mr. Owl said hello in a gentle voice. He showed them where to hang their coats and where to sit. He showed them where to find the bathroom and offered everyone a piece of fruit.

Then, Beaver and Bear went to the reading and writing center. Rabbit went to the play kitchen. But Franklin stayed in his seat.

"What would you like to do today, Franklin?" asked Mr. Owl.

"I don't know," said Franklin, rubbing his tummy. "I cannot write all the numbers like Rabbit can. I cannot read like Beaver can."

"Rabbit and Beaver will learn new things at school, and so will you."

Franklin started to doodle.

"I can see that you are a very good artist," said the teacher.

Franklin sat up taller. "I know all my colors, too," he said.

"What color is this?" asked Mr. Owl, holding up a colored pencil.

"It's a special blue," said Franklin. "It is turquoise."

"Now you have taught *me* something," said Mr. Owl. "Is there something special *you* would like to learn?"

There were so many things Franklin wanted to learn that he had trouble deciding.

Finally, he asked Mr. Owl to help him read his favorite book.

Franklin made a building of blocks.

He sorted the money in the classroom store and painted four pictures. One for the teacher, one for himself and two for his parents.

It was a wonderful day.

Franklin sat at the back of the bus all the way home. He bumped up and down. He was so busy having fun that he almost forgot to get off at his stop.

His parents were waiting. "How is your tummy?" they asked.

Franklin looked puzzled. It had been such a good day that he had forgotten all about his jumpy tummy.

"My tummy is empty!" he said.

"That's a feeling that will go away, too," said Franklin's father.

165

"I made this for you," said Franklin's mother. She gave Franklin his favorite snack, fly pie.

"And I made this for you," said Franklin. He gave his parents two pictures and two big hugs.

Franklin's School Play

FRANKLIN could count forwards and backwards. He could remember his phone number, his address and the names of six different shapes. But sometimes Franklin was forgetful. So he worried when Mr. Owl chose him to play one of the lead roles in the class play. What if he forgot his lines?

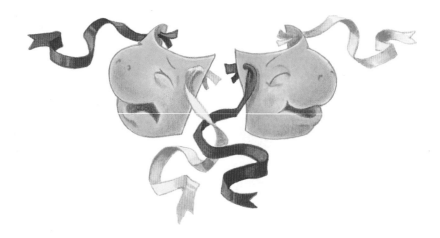

Every December, Mr. Owl's students put on a show that they made up themselves. This year they would perform A Salute to the Nutcracker.

Franklin had seen the Nutcracker ballet with his parents, and he'd listened to the music at home. He loved the story about a little girl and the toy soldier who comes to life.

Franklin had a big part to learn. At home he said his lines over and over again.

"I hope I don't forget what to say," he told his parents.

They encouraged him. "If you practice, you'll be fine."

Franklin wasn't so sure.

173

174

The week before the show, there was a flurry of activity in the classroom.

Everyone had an important job to do.

Goose studied her lines. Beaver practiced her ballet steps. The musicians learned their songs.

"Lovely! Lovely!" said Mr. Owl.

Raccoon was in charge of building the sets. His team had already cut, glued, painted and decorated most of the scenery. Now they were busy trimming the tree. Mr. Owl thought it was spectacular.

Bear was the costume designer. He and his friends created wonderful costumes with bits of this and that.

When Mr. Owl saw what they had made, he clapped and said, "Delightful!"

The cast practiced speaking loudly and clearly.
Badger was the stage manager so she prompted the
players when they couldn't remember their lines.
"That's great," said Mr. Owl. "But where is Franklin?"
Raccoon pointed to the art supply cupboard.

Franklin peeked out. "I need a quiet place to learn my lines," he said. "I get to the middle and then I forget."

"Let's work on them together," suggested Mr. Owl.

By the end of the day, Franklin could say his lines without missing a word.

"Bravo!" said Mr. Owl.

184

It was the day before the show. The programs were printed and the seats were set up. For the first time, the students would practice on stage. Mr. Owl directed everyone to their places.

Rabbit thumped his feet in excitement.

"Quiet please," said Mr. Owl. "Curtain time."

Franklin went over the lines in his head.

The curtain opened. Franklin was silent.
Mr. Owl whispered, "It's time to begin."
Franklin tried to talk, but his throat was
tight. Every time he looked at the empty seats,
he was scared.

"Psst," said Badger. "I'll tell you what to say."
But Franklin didn't need a prompter. He
remembered the lines. He just couldn't say
them out loud.

Mr. Owl talked to Franklin alone.

"Maybe you have stage fright," said Mr. Owl. "Try not to think about the audience."

Franklin tried three more times. But each time the curtain opened, Franklin's mouth stayed closed.

He didn't want to give up, but they were running out of time. So Franklin asked Mr. Owl if he could switch places with Badger. She could play the Nutcracker Prince because she knew all the lines.

189

190

They started again. Badger couldn't be heard at the back of the room.

Mr. Owl nudged Franklin. "Why don't you help her out."

Franklin stood on stage beside Badger. "Try saying your lines like this."

Franklin spoke in a booming voice. He meant to say just one line. But Franklin got carried away and said a whole speech.

When he was finished, everyone cheered.

"You got over your stage fright!" said Mr. Owl.

"I guess I did," laughed Franklin.

Badger looked relieved.

The next night, when the curtain opened,
Franklin saw his family sitting in the front row.
He took a deep breath.

Franklin's first words were soft and raspy.
Keep going, he told himself. And he did. Franklin
acted so well that he almost believed he really
was the Nutcracker Prince.

It was a marvellous show. After the finale,
the audience gave the class a standing ovation.
Franklin and his friends bowed four times.

And that night, after a hot cocoa by the fire,
Franklin pasted the show program into his scrapbook.
It was a night he wanted to remember forever.

Franklin's Class Trip

FRANKLIN could count by twos and tie his shoes. He had gone with his class to the bakery, the fire station and the pet store. Today Franklin's class was going to the museum. Franklin was so excited that he could hardly eat his breakfast.

The museum had lots of steps and huge doors.
"Wow, it's big," said Franklin.
"It has to be," said Beaver. "There are real dinosaurs inside."

Beaver had been to the museum before. She knew everything about it.

"*Big* dinosaurs," she emphasized. "So big that they ate trees for breakfast."

Franklin was afraid to ask what dinosaurs ate for lunch.

203

Franklin sat down on the steps.

"What's wrong?" asked Snail.

"Beaver says there are real dinosaurs in the museum."

Snail looked alarmed. "That sounds scary."

Franklin nodded.

In the museum lobby, Mr. Owl went over the rules. No shouting. No running. And stay with the group.

"Mr. Owl," said Beaver, "one more thing. Watch out for dinosaurs."

Moose and Bear laughed.

Franklin didn't. He moved a little closer to Mr. Owl.

Their first stop was the bat cave.

It was dark inside. Squeaks and squawks filled the air.

"What's that?" asked Franklin.

Beaver giggled. "That's the sound bats make to find their way around."

Franklin was relieved that it was bats and not dinosaurs.

209

The class visited the rain forest next.
Franklin climbed high into a tree house.
He could see the tops of trees.
"Can you spot any dinosaurs?" asked Snail.
Franklin shook his head and climbed
down quickly.

There was so much to do in the museum that Franklin almost forgot about the dinosaurs.

In the medieval room, Franklin had fun dressing up like a knight.

Franklin even got to dig in a sandy pit.
He was the first one to find an arrowhead.
It was just like being a real archaeologist.

"The best part is still to come," said Beaver
as they sat down in the cafeteria.

"Yes," agreed Bear. "Lunch!"

Mr. Owl smiled. "I think Beaver means the
dinosaur exhibit."

Franklin gulped. "I'm too tired to see more.
I'll just stay here for a while," he muttered.

"Me too," said Snail.

"You'll forget about being tired when you see
the dinosaurs," said Mr. Owl. "Eat up and let's go."

217

Reluctantly, Franklin and Snail followed
giant footprints down a long, leafy corridor.
There was a loud roar. The floor shook.
So did Franklin.

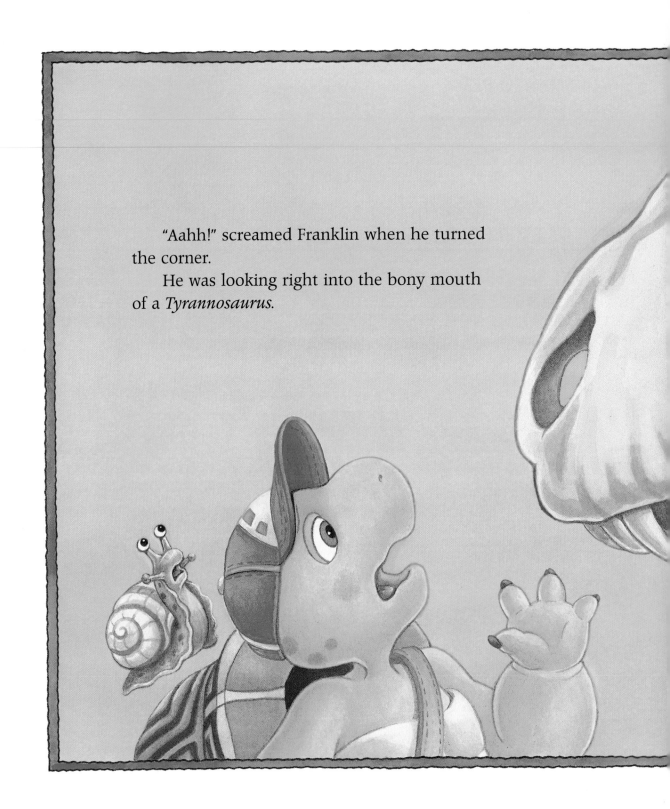

"Aahh!" screamed Franklin when he turned the corner.

He was looking right into the bony mouth of a *Tyrannosaurus*.

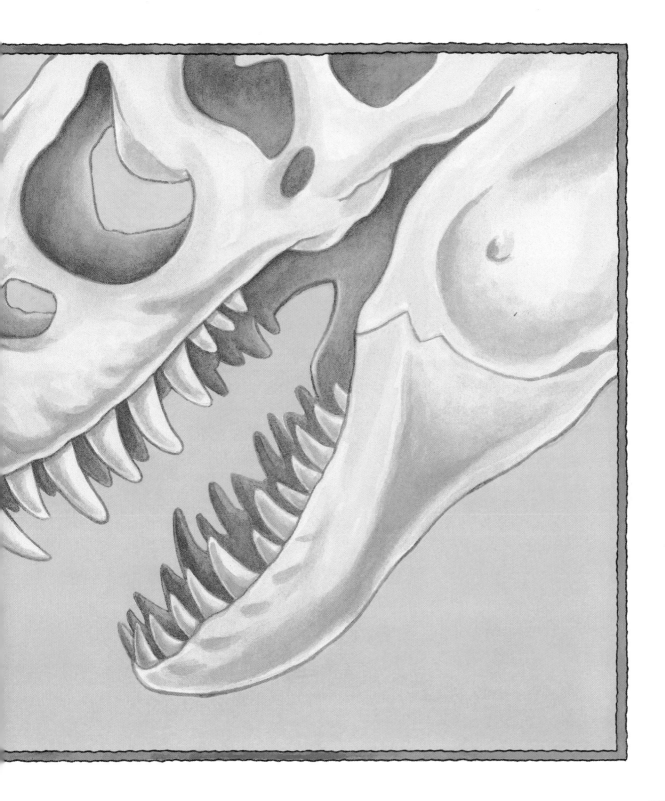

Franklin blinked. "They're bones! Real dinosaur bones! But the dinosaurs aren't alive."

"Alive?" giggled Beaver. "Of course not. There hasn't been a live dinosaur for millions of years. You make good jokes, Franklin."

"You sure do," whispered Snail.

As they were leaving, Franklin and his friends walked past the Egyptian exhibit.

"Next time," said Beaver, "you should visit the tomb. There's a mummy inside."

"Is it real?" asked Franklin.

"Yes, and scary," said Beaver.

But Franklin wasn't scared. He had a mummy at home.

And he could hardly wait to tell her all
about his adventures at the museum.

Franklin's Neighborhood

FRANKLIN could count to ten and back again and say the alphabet without stopping. He liked drawing pictures and he loved show and tell. So when Mr. Owl assigned the first project of the year, Franklin was ready.

"We live in a neighborhood," explained Mr. Owl. "And our neighborhood is made up of houses and stores and —"

"Gardens," said Snail.

"And a hospital," added Badger.

"Exactly!" said Mr. Owl. "Now, for tomorrow, I want each of you to draw a picture of what you like best about our neighborhood."

"What do you like best?" asked Franklin.

Mr. Owl thought for a moment.

"The school," he replied.

Everyone laughed.

When Franklin got home, he hurried to his room.
"Do you want a snack?" asked his mother.
"No thanks," said Franklin. "I have a project to do."

Franklin took out his crayons and some paper. Then he sat down to think.

He thought about the ice cream store, then the bicycle trail, and then the soccer field.

Franklin sighed. Choosing the best thing about his neighborhood was not going to be easy.

Franklin went to find his mother.

"Could I have that snack now, please?" he asked. "I think my brain is hungry."

But after three fly cookies and two glasses of milk, Franklin still hadn't decided what he liked best.

"Why don't you go for a walk around the neighborhood?" suggested his mother.

"That might help," said Franklin. He got his paper and crayons and off he went.

Franklin met Beaver in the meadow.

"I've finished my project," Beaver announced. "I picked the library, and I went there right after school to draw my picture."

Franklin thought about storytime with Mrs. Goose, the librarian.

"That's a good idea," Franklin said. "Maybe that's what I'll draw."

He waved good-bye and headed for the library.

Franklin was sitting on the library steps when Fox came by.

"Have you finished your project?" asked Fox.

Franklin shook his head. "I was going to draw the library, but on the way here I saw the movie theater. I can't make up my mind."

"I chose the fire station," said Fox.

Franklin remembered the time Chief Wolf let him sit in the fire truck.

"That's a good idea," Franklin said. "Maybe that's what I'll draw."

He collected his paper and crayons and set off.

Franklin was outside the fire station when he saw Moose.

"Have you finished your project?" asked Moose.

"No," Franklin sighed. "I was going to draw the fire station, but on the way here I saw other places I like just as much."

"I like the pond best of all," said Moose.

Franklin thought about swimming and skating with his friends.

"That's a good idea," Franklin answered. "Maybe that's what I'll draw."

He said good-bye and headed for the pond.

Franklin was staring at the water when Bear came along.

"What's the matter?" asked Bear.

"I can't decide what to draw for my project," said Franklin. "I like too many things."

"My best place is the berry patch," said Bear.

Franklin thought about all the times he and Bear had picked berries together.

"See?" said Franklin. "Another great idea!"

"What about the park?" Bear suggested.

Franklin thought about playing with his friends on the swings and slide.

"That's it!" declared Franklin.

He said good-bye to Bear and hurried off.

Franklin's mother found him sitting alone on the teeter-totter.

"Did the walk help?" she asked.

"Not really," replied Franklin. "There are so many great things in our neighborhood."

Franklin's mother gave him a hug.

"Let's go home and talk," she said. "I made your favorite supper."

Franklin grinned. "At least I know what *that* is!"

Franklin felt a bit better after broccoli soup and fly pie.

"I'm ready to think again," he said. Then he asked his parents what they liked best about the neighborhood.

"I like the farmers market on Saturday mornings," said his mother.

Franklin smiled. He loved Farmer Rabbit's sweet peas and Farmer Squirrel's fly brownies.

"And I like belonging to my chess club," said his father.

Franklin agreed. He liked belonging to the chess club, too.

249

Then Franklin remembered something.

"Is it true that Mr. Heron is moving?" he asked. Mr. Heron was the president of the chess club.

"Yes, it is true," replied Franklin's father. "I'm going to miss him very much. This neighborhood won't be the same without him."

251

Franklin nodded. He was going to miss
Mr. Heron, too.

Suddenly Franklin knew what he wanted
to draw.

"I know what I like best!" he said.

Franklin ran to his room and started working.

At school the next day, everyone was
excited. It was time to see the projects.

Raccoon went first. "I drew the river," he said.

"I drew the forest," said Hawk.

Finally, it was Franklin's turn. He unrolled
a huge sheet of paper.

It was covered with drawings of almost everyone that Franklin knew. "I don't get it," said Beaver.

Franklin smiled.

"I drew my neighbors," he said. "That's what
I like best about my neighborhood."